Time for Bed, Little Chick

Written by Mary Packard
Illustrated by Carolyn Ewing

LEVEL **1** READER
READING LEVEL
PRE K – GRADE 1

Dalmatian Press

CE13159/1012

"It's time for bed!"
called Mama Hen.
Little Chick wanted to keep playing.

Chickita and Chester
brushed their beaks.
But did Little Chick?

"Vroom! Vroom!"

"What are you doing?"
asked Mama Hen.

"My toothbrush is an airplane,"
said Little Chick.

"Then fly it around your beak,"
said Mama Hen.

Little Chick looked outside.
Baby Owl was just waking up.
Kitten was chasing Firefly.

"I wish I could stay up late," he said.
"It's no fun being a chicken.
 No fun at all!"

Chickita and Chester
combed their feathers,
"What good chicks you are!"
chirped Mama Hen.

But did Little Chick comb his feathers?
"La la la la," he sang.
"I'm playing a song on my comb.
 Let's sing!"

Chickita and Chester
put on their pajamas.

But Little Chick waved
his pajamas in the air.
"I'm a bullfighter," he said.
"Watch out for the bull!"

"Watch out for *me*!"
giggled Mama Hen.
"Or I'll scoop you up
and plop you into bed!"

Mama Hen read her three
chicks a bedtime story.
She kissed them goodnight.

Two chicks fell asleep.
But one chick did not.

Mama Hen went to bed.
She heard some chirping.
"Mama! I'm thirsty," it said.

Mama took Little Chick
a glass of water.
Then she went back to bed.

Mama pulled her covers up.
And she heard more chirping.
"What is it this time?" she asked.

"I'm not tired," said Little Chick.
"Please tell me one more story."
"All right," said Mama. "Just one."

*Once upon a time there lived
a sweet little baby chick.
He had soft, fluffy feathers.*

(He looked a lot like you.)

This baby chick loved to play,
but he always went to bed on time.

And do you know why?

Because he knew that some day he would grow up to be a big, handsome rooster.

*Roosters go to bed before
the sun sets, you know.
And they get up before
sunrise each day.*

They sing cock-a-doodle-doo
to wake everyone on the farm.

"Won't that be a fun job,
Little Chick?" asked Mama.

"Little Chick?"

Mama Hen smiled.
"Goodnight, Little Chick.
Sleep tight."